Bible Stories
with
Songs & Fingerplays

Collected from over 10 years of the respected Christian education curriculum and worship resource *The Whole People of God*, these volumes offer tried and true material in easy-to-use format. These are proven resources with a theology and approach that thousands have come to trust.

Bible Stories

WITH SONGS & FINGERPLAYS

Compiled by Julie Elliot

Illustrated by Crystal Przybille

WOOD LAKE BOOKS

Editor: Cheryl Perry
Cover design and cover art: Margaret Kyle
Interior design: Julie Bachewich
Consulting art director: Robert MacDonald
Cover photo: Dan Mawson, Photographic Resources

At Wood Lake Books, we practice what we publish, guided by a concern for fairness, justice, and equal opportunity in all of our relationships with employees and customers.

We acknowledge the financial support of the Government of Canada through the Book Publishing Industry Development Program for our publishing activities.

Canadian Cataloguing in Publication Data
Elliot, Julie, 1959–
Bible stories with songs and fingerplays
Includes index.
ISBN 1-55145-297-9
1. Bible stories, English. I. Przybille, Crystal. II. Perry, Cheryl, 1970– III. Title.
BS551.2.E44 1998 j220.9'505 C98-910157-6

Printing 10 9 8 7 6 5 4 3 2 1

Published by Wood Lake Books
Kelowna, British Columbia, Canada

Printed in Canada by
Cariboo Press, Vernon, British Columbia

Table of Contents

Stories from the Hebrew Scriptures

Stories from the Greek Scriptures

Musical Scores

A Note from the Compiler

Young children love stories! They always like hearing their favorites – whether from parents, grandparents, children's books, television, videos, or story time at preschool and kindergarten. But chances are, they aren't hearing many Bible stories. Why not? Most children's Bibles are too complicated for them, and many parents find it challenging to tell the stories in a simple yet rich enough way to hold their young child's attention. But children need to hear Bible stories at this early age and they need to hear them often. Even if they're regularly attending church school, chances are Walt Disney still has more influence in shaping the way our children first understand the world. If you have trouble believing this, ask a few four-year-olds to tell you everything they know about Snow White and the Seven Dwarfs. Then ask them to tell you everything they know about Jesus. It's tough to compete!

Bible Stories with Songs and Fingerplays offers an alternative. From ten years of the popular *Whole People of God* curriculum, we have gathered simple tellings of some of the best-known, best-loved Bible stories – simple tellings that retain the richness and drama of the original stories. Some stories encourage participation. Simple songs, poems and fingerplays are included to reinforce the story and help children "live into the story" through imagination and fun.

This kind of storytelling will have children making connections between what they know from the Bible and what is happening in their day-to-day lives. Storytime becomes theology as children shape ideas about who God is and what God wants for us and our world. We hope this book will help introduce your children to stories they will encounter over and over as they grow – and never tire of hearing!

JULIE ELLIOT

How to Use *Bible Stories with Songs and Fingerplays*

We hope that this book will be read at home and that it will be useful for programs where a group of children are assembled (e.g. Sunday School, mid-week groups, summer programs, Bible camps). The section at the beginning of the book called "Stages of Development – 3-, 4- and 5-year-olds" will be particularly useful for teachers in group situations. Stories include suggestions for storytellers. The fold-out cover includes figures children can cut out and use to retell stories. Illustrations throughout the book may be colored with your child's help to make this first book of Bible stories even more meaningful.

Stages of Development (Three-Year-Olds)
Observable Responses and Implications for Teachers and Parents

Mental Development

- Three-year-olds ask questions constantly, accept logical explanations, and investigate everything.
- Preschoolers are increasingly interested in things they can do with their hands. They can match simple forms (e.g. circles, triangles, etc.) and are interested in color.
- Preschoolers are starting to learn words. Many will have good working vocabularies. They speak in sentences, many of which are questions. Encourage children to express ideas verbally.
- Young children like the same stories and pictures over and over. They like simple stories about familiar things, especially narratives about themselves. Repeat. Repeat. Repeat. Have fun with words, unusual sounds, rhymes, and stories.
- Three-year-olds have short attention spans. They remember isolated episodes of stories, but may not be ready to think in logical progression. Take into account children's limitations. Let them set their own pace.

Physical Development

- Three-year-olds have fairly good hand coordination. They can hold crayons as adults do instead of in their fists. They use some finger motions instead of scribbling with their whole arm in motion. They enjoy fingerplays and songs with actions that make use of this new-found coordination.
- Three-year-olds are comparatively nearsighted and will want to hold pictures and books in order to see them.

Stages of Development (Four-Year-Olds)
Observable Responses and Implications for Teachers and Parents

Mental Development

- Four-year-olds can be very active, noisy, and they move from one activity to another quickly. Space to move around in is helpful. Move from active participation to quiet participation and back again. Songs and fingerplays are helpful here. Story conversations should not last more than 5 – 7 minutes.
- Young children like the same stories and pictures over and over. They like simple stories about familiar things, especially narratives about themselves. Repeat. Repeat. Repeat. Have fun with words, unusual sounds, rhymes, and stories.
- Four-year-olds see a part of something or the whole thing. They do not see the relationship between the part and the whole. Ask "what" and "when" and "who" questions. "Why" questions are difficult for this age group.

- Preschoolers are starting to learn words. Many will have good working vocabularies. They speak in sentences and express ideas verbally. Use stories to build vocabulary and introduce concepts.
- Four-year-olds need security, attention, and affirmation. Children like repetition. Keep routines simple and don't change them often. Set limits for behavior expression and be consistent.

Physical Development

- Four-year-olds are developing large muscles, but still lack much small muscle control. Don't expect children to be able to tie bows or cut well with scissors.

Stages of Development (Five-Year-Olds)
Observable Responses and Implications for Teachers and Parents

Mental Development

- Five-year-olds can concentrate for longer periods of time. Story conversation time can usually last up to 10 minutes.
- Five-year-olds can remember simple routines. They are learning to take turns and ask for things. Encourage children to do more things for themselves. Offer them some choices.
- Five-year-olds are beginning to arrange things in a series. They can make simple comparisons. Expect more during story conversations. Get them to compare stories to their own experience.
- Some children at this age can print their own names. They enjoy learning fingerplays, rhyming poems, and rhythm-action verses. They can memorize words to simple songs.
- Five-year-olds fluctuate between fantasy and reality. Daydreaming, pretending, and play are important ways for them to explore and learn. Have them act out or "be" the story.

Physical Development

- Five-year-olds are developing large muscles and have much better small muscle control than four-year-olds. They can cut, paste, tie bows and draw recognizable pictures.

Spiritual Development of Three-, Four-, and Five-Year-Olds

Religious or Theological Needs of Children

- Children need freedom to make their own decisions about God. God grants this freedom; adults must do so, too.
- Children will come to know God through other people in relationships in which they can experience love, forgiveness, discipline, security and self-esteem.
- Children's faith will be based on concepts or ideals. Facts only serve as a means by which concepts are formulated.
- Children need to be able to develop their own faith at their own pace.
- Children need to see a wholeness to their lives and realize that religion is not isolated but is a part of this wholeness.
- Children need to have confidence in themselves, in God, and in others. This is faith.
- Very young children especially need to feel a sense of trust in those who care for them.
- Children need to feel that they are part of the church now and not going through a waiting or apprentice period.
- When we speak of being made "in the image of God" we are speaking of self-respect. This develops as children are affirmed in their own personhood and enabled to see themselves as unique persons.
- Children need to see themselves as children of God who follow Jesus Christ, our teacher and leader, into God's realm.

Religious Thinking of Young Children

"When I was a child, my speech, feelings, and thinking were all those of a child."
1 Corinthians 13:11

Abstract thinking is not possible for young children, so God and Jesus often seem the same to them. By showing pictures and telling stories about Jesus, they begin to know Jesus as a loving person.

Questions about God are best answered in a simple, truthful manner. Affirm for children that God is the creator of the natural wonders which they are just discovering, and that God loves them very much.

Homemade Musical Instruments

Tambourine

Tambourines were played when people gathered together to celebrate or worship.

Place some pebbles or beans between two paper plates and staple or tape together face-to-face. Punch holes and tie some bells around the edge of the plates. Tape streamers to one edge. Tap the sides of the tambourine with your hands or shake it.

Kazoo

Humming into these makes a great sound!

Cover the end of a cardboard tube with wax paper and secure it with a rubber band. Punch a hole with a pencil near covered end.

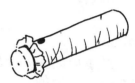

Panpipes

Cut three or four drinking straws to different lengths. Lay a strip of tape on a flat surface sticky-side-up. Align the ends of six or eight straws as you place them onto a piece of tape. Put another strip of tape over the straws to hold them in place. Experiment with blowing gently over the tops of the straws.

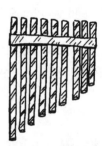

Bell Shaker

Thread a piece of yarn through a jingle bell and tie. Then tape loop to a thick cardboard tube. Do this with several bells. Hold the tube and shake.

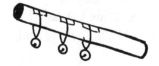

Balloon Shaker

Pour a small amount of rice, sand, or beans into a deflated balloon. Inflate the balloon and tie it closed. Shake!

Plastic Jug

This creates a wonderful sound and is so easy! It's obtaining the jugs that might be difficult.

You will need a large plastic jug (bottled water is sold in these large, clear plastic containers) and yarn. If you wish, create a colorful pattern on the jug by winding several rows of thick yarn around the base of it (or braid the yarn first). Hold the jug between the legs or under one arm and use palms of hands to beat a rhythm.

Nail Triangle

Tie a short length of string to a large nail. Hold the nail by the string and strike it with another nail to make triangle sounds.

Log Drum

Early people found out that beating a hollow log made more sound than beating a solid log.

You will need two large juice cans with both ends removed, strong tape (e.g. duct tape) and two sticks (e.g. chopsticks). Tape the cans together to form a "log." If you wish, cover the cans with brown paper and decorate with markers. Strike drum with the sticks to create sounds.

Plastic Bottle Shaker

Use a clean plastic jar or bottle with a lid. Put beads, popping corn, or pebbles inside the jar. Place white glue around the inside rim of the jar and tighten lid to seal.

Sandpaper Rhythm Sticks

Wrap pieces of fine or medium weight sandpaper around wooden dowels. Glue the edges in place. Rub the sticks together to make an interesting sound.

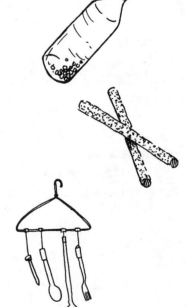

Coat Hanger Chimes

Suspend various items from a coat hanger (e.g. large spoon, small flower pot, nail, fork). Tap them with a spoon or other metal object.

Stories
from the
Hebrew Scriptures

God Makes a World

Genesis 1:1–2:4a

Children will pick up the pattern of the story very quickly. As you tell it, pause after "and God said…"
and let them complete the phrase "that's good!"

Long, long, long ago, before there was anything, before there was a
world, before there was light, before there was darkness, there was God.
Just God. All alone.
So God decided to make the world.
Then God said, "Let there be light."
So there was.
Beautiful light shining everywhere.
And God said, **"That's good."**
Then God said, "Let there be a sky above, and water
below."
So there was.
And God said, **"That's good."**

Then God said, "Let there be green plants and tall
trees and grass and beautiful flowers. And let them
all make seeds so there can be new plants when the
old ones die."
So there were.
And God said, **"That's good."**
Then God said, "Let there be a golden sun in
the sky in the daytime, and a silver moon at
night."
So there was.
And God said, **"That's good."**
Then God said, "Let there be all kinds of shiny fish
in the sea and bright colored birds to fly in the air. And
let the fish have baby fish, and the birds have baby birds,
so there can always be new birds and fish when the old
ones die."
So there were.
And God said, **"That's good."**
Then God said, "Let there be animals on the land. All kinds
of animals that run and crawl and gallop."
So there were.
And God said, **"That's good."**

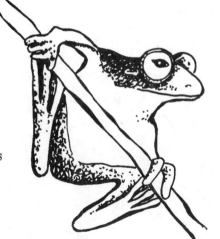

Then God said, "Let there be people in the world, and let the people be made so they are like me." So God created people. Women and men. And God said to the people, "Let there be new babies born so there will always be new people in the world when the old people die."

Then God said to the people, "Take care of my world. It's yours to use. All of it. But please be kind to my world."

Then God looked at the world, and all the beautiful things in it. And God said, **"That's *very* good."**

When it was all done, God rested.

from *The Family Story Bible* ©1996 Northstone Publishing, Inc.

God Is Great

(tune: Twinkle, Twinkle Little Star)
God made the sun to warm us all *(make a circle with arms above head)*
God is great! God is great!
God made the night with stars so bright *(wiggle fingers like stars twinkling)*
God is great! God is great!
God made me *(point to self)*
and God made you *(point to others)*
God loves us,
We love God, too! *(hug self)*

I Feel Happy Now

(tune: Kum Ba Yah)
I feel happy now,
Thank you, God. *(fold hands in prayer)*
I feel loved by you, *(hug self)*
Thank you, God.
I'm the only one *(hold up one finger)*
just like me. *(point to self)*
I'm a special gift from God.

Here Is My Mouth

Here is my mouth, my fingers, my toes *(point to mouth, wiggle fingers and toes)*
Here is my chest, my knees and my nose *(cross hands over chest, touch knees and nose)*
All of these parts make a wonderful me! *(hands start at the feet and move up the body)*
What a great gift to others I can be!

God Made the Birds

God made the birds *(flutter hands)*
God made the bees *(make zzzzz sound)*
God made the sun *(make a circle with arms above head)*
God made the trees *(stretch out arms)*
Look all around and you will see,
that God made you *(point to others)*
and God made me. *(point to self)*
Thank you, God.

God Made the Animals

God made the animals *(crouch like a frog)*
God made the trees *(stand tall like trees)*
But best of all,
God made me! *(point to self)*

Noah Sees a Rainbow

Genesis 6:9–9:17

Children will enjoy participating in the telling of this story by acting out the words in italics.

God told Noah, "A very, very big rain is coming. Water will cover everything. You must build a big boat so your family and all the animals will be safe."

Noah and his wife and their children began to build a big boat, called an ark. They sawed the wood *(make sawing motion)* and hammered the nails *(pretend to pound nails)*. When the boat was good and strong, they climbed in and began to call the animals.

Cows came first *(make sound)* and pigs *(make sound)* and dogs *(make sound)* and crows *(make sound)* and bees *(make sound)* and quiet little mice *(shh … hold finger to lips)*. Two of every kind of animal came into the ark. Then the door was shut.

It was very quiet. Everyone waited. Then they heard it. Drip, drop, drip, drop *(pat knees slowly)*. The rain began. Drip, drop, drip, drop *(pat knees faster)*. Soon the boat was floating. Gentle waves rocked the ark back and forth *(rock back and forth)*. It rained for a very long time.

Then one day it was quiet again. They listened. The rain had stopped! Noah and his family were so happy they jumped up and down and cheered *(shout "Hurray!")*. The sun came out and dried up all the water. Noah and his family climbed out of the boat. They stood on dry land and spread out their arms to enjoy the sunshine. Then the animals came out two by two. There were cows *(make sound)* and pigs *(make sound)* and dogs *(make sound)* and crows *(make sound)* and bees *(make sound)* and quiet little mice *(shh … hold finger to lips)*.

Noah and his family looked around and saw that everything was different. They knew they had to start over again. They knelt down on the ground to say thank you to God for the dry land, the warm sun, the growing plants and the animals. They folded their hands and bowed their heads to say *(fold hands and bow heads)* "Thank you, God, for giving us everything we need to start over!" Then they looked up at the sky and saw the most beautiful rainbow. The rainbow was a sign of God's promise to Noah and all the plants and animals and us – that God will never stop loving or caring for us.

God's Rainbow

(tune: Three Blind Mice)

God's rainbow, God's rainbow
See it glow, see it glow
It tells us all about God's promise,
to love us and always take care of us.
The sign in the sky that tells us this
is God's rainbow, God's rainbow.

> Do you know the colors of the rainbow? They are top to bottom: red, orange, yellow, green, blue, purple.

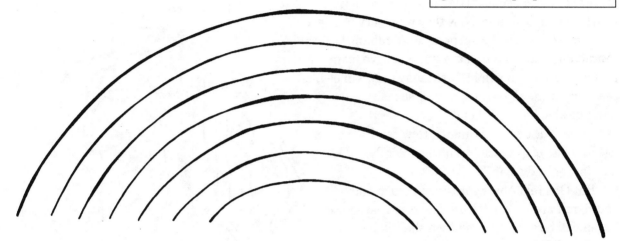

Noah and His Family

(tune: Itsy Bitsy Spider)

Noah and his family built a great big boat.
Down came the rain, the ark began to float.
Out came the sun to dry up all the rain,
And in the sky a rainbow, to say "Let's start again."

A Rainbow

From big, black clouds *(shape clouds with arms above head)*
The raindrops come *(wiggle fingers like falling rain)*.
Drip, drip, drip they fall,
Until God's sun *(make large circle with hands)*
Shines through each one
And makes a rainbow tall *(arms above head in an arch)*.

God Surprises Abraham and Sarah

Genesis 17:4-7, 15-16, 21:1-7

Make towel dolls with young children. Use these to tell the story.

Abraham and Sarah were a small family who loved God very much. They had been married for a long, long time. But they had never had any children. Now they were very old.

One day, God had a surprise for Abraham. God said, "Abraham, you and Sarah are going to have many grandchildren. You will have so many they will be like the stars in the sky – there will be so many you won't be able to count them!"

"What?" thought Abraham. "How can I have lots and lots of grandchildren when Sarah and I have never had a baby?"

But God told Abraham, "Even though you and Sarah are very old, I will make you parents. Sarah will be a mother and then she will be a grandmother to many, many children."

Abraham and Sarah were so happy about God's surprise that they both laughed. They were not sure how it could happen, but they trusted God's promise.

Soon Sarah and Abraham had a son. They named him Isaac. Even though they were old they found God gave them the strength to be good parents and enjoy their baby.

Sarah said, "God helps us to do things we could never do on our own. I could never imagine being a mother in my old age. I did it with God's help. I wonder what other exciting things God has in store for us?"

Abraham and Sarah knew their lives were going to be very different from now on. Only one thing was going to be the same. God would be with them just as God had always been with them, loving them and caring for them.

God Keeps Promises

(tune: Paw Paw Patch)

1. Abraham and Sarah wanted a baby *(3x)*
   God sent them baby Isaac to love.

2. God kept the promise to Abraham and Sarah *(3x)*
   (Yes) God sent them baby Isaac to love.

3. God has promised always to love us *(3x)*
   Jesus helps us all to know God's love.

4. Jesus has promised to be with us *(3x)*
   And help us walk in God's loving way.

Wait and Hope

(tune: Row, Row, Row Your Boat)
Wait, wait, wait and hope,
God's promise would come true.
Wait, wait, wait and hope,
That's all that they could do.

Yes, yes, yes it did –
God's promise did come true.
God gave them a baby boy,
Just as God promised to.

Celebrating the Promise

(tune: Ring around the Rosy)
You're going to be a mother (*or* father)
You're going to be a mother
Praise God, Praise God
Prai-se God! *(lift hands together)*
(Join hands in a circle. Choose someone to be
Sarah or Abraham and invite them to stand
inside the circle and pretend to rock a baby.
Continue until everyone has had a chance to be
Sarah or Abraham.)

Towel Dolls

Here's a simple doll to make from a bath towel.

1. Lay towel flat (Fig. 1).
2. Roll each side to the middle (Fig. 2).
3. Fold rolled towel in half (Fig. 3).
4. Tie head tightly with string (Fig. 4).
5. Pull one side up over head and then roll sides
   down to form arms (Fig. 5).

Fig. 1   Fig. 2   Fig. 3   Fig. 4   Fig. 5

Naomi and Ruth

Ruth 1:1-22

Naomi lived in Bethlehem. Once there was no rain in Bethlehem for a long time, so there wasn't enough food for everyone to eat. Naomi and her family moved to another country called Moab where there was food. They lived there for a little while. Then something sad happened. Naomi's husband and two sons died. Naomi had only two people left in her family – Ruth and Orpah. Naomi decided to go back to Bethlehem. But she didn't want to leave Ruth and Orpah behind. They said, "Please don't go without us, Naomi. We love you and want to be with you." So the three women set out together. They walked and walked and walked.

After they had traveled for awhile, Naomi said, "Are you sure you should come with me? I think it would be better for you to stay in Moab with your parents. Moab is where you belong." Orpah thought about what Naomi said. She loved Naomi, but she missed her parents. She decided to stay in Moab. Orpah hugged Ruth and Naomi. She said goodbye. Then she turned around and went back to her parents' home.

Ruth decided she would stay with Naomi. She said, "Please don't tell me to leave you. I will go where you go. I will live where you live. We will always be together!"

Naomi and Ruth continued on their walk to Bethlehem. It was a long, long walk. They had to cross some dry, rocky land. The sun was hot. There was little food and water but they shared what they had. At times they felt afraid and they held hands to make each other feel brave. At times they felt lonely and sang songs to cheer each other up. Ruth told funny stories that made Naomi laugh. Naomi rubbed Ruth's sore back when they stopped to rest under a tree. Even missing Orpah was easier because they had each other to say, "Yes, I miss her, too." Every morning and every night they prayed together. They knew that God was always with them. Finally they arrived in Bethlehem. The whole town was excited to see them. They welcomed the women with hugs and kisses and said, "Welcome! Welcome! We're glad to have you here with us!"

Choices

(tune: Row, Row, Row Your Boat)
Choices, choices,
are very hard to make.
God will be there all the way
and bless each step we take.

If You're Happy

If you're happy and you know it clap your hands *(clap clap)*.
If you're happy and you know it clap your hands *(clap clap)*.
If you're happy and you know, then your face will surely show it.
If you're happy and you know it clap your hands *(clap clap)*.

Other verses:
If you're loving and you feel it throw a kiss...
If you're excited and you feel it give a jump...
If you're sad and you feel it cry boo hoo...
If you're angry and you feel it stamp your foot...
If you're proud and you feel it stand up tall...
If you're tired and you feel it give a yawn...
If you're relaxed and you feel it flop around...
If you're happy and you feel it hug a friend...

God Calls Samuel by Name

1 Samuel 3:1-18

To make a pop-up puppet of Samuel to tell this story, see the instructions on the next page. As you tell the story, bend the puppet up each time Samuel hears his name being called.

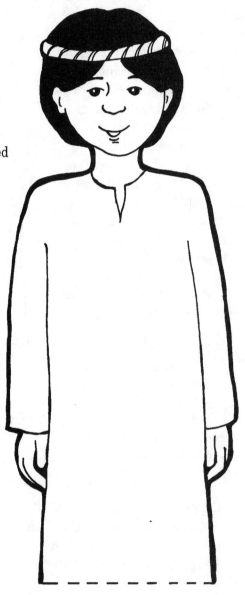

There was a boy named Samuel. Samuel lived in the temple with a priest named Eli *(pronounced Ee-lie)*. The temple was where the Jewish people went to worship. Samuel was a helper for Eli because Eli was old and couldn't see very well. One night Samuel was lying in bed and he heard someone call his name. "Samuel! Samuel!" *(Bend the puppet up.)*

Samuel went to see Eli and said, "Here I am. You called me."

Eli was puzzled. "I didn't call you. Go back to bed."

So, Samuel went back to bed. *(Bend the puppet back.)* He thought he must have been dreaming. Then he heard someone call him again. "Samuel! Samuel! *(Bend the puppet up.)*

He went to Eli again and said, "Here I am. You called me."

Eli shook his head. "I didn't call you, child. Go back to bed." *(Bend the puppet back.)*

Samuel was confused but he went back to bed again and tried to sleep. Again, he heard someone call his name. "Samuel! Samuel!" *(Bend the puppet up.)*

He went to Eli again and said, "Yes, Eli, it must be you calling me. Here I am!"

Eli finally understood that it must be God calling Samuel. Eli said, "If you hear your name again, you must say, 'Yes, God. I am listening'." *(Bend the puppet back.)*

Samuel was excited and a little afraid. He went back to bed. Then he heard someone call his name again. *(Bend the puppet up.)* He answered. "Yes, God, I am listening." Then God gave Samuel an important message to give to Eli. In the morning Samuel gave the message to Eli, just as God asked him to do.

God Calls Us

(tune: Hey La-di, La-di, La-di)
God calls us, calls us, calls us
God calls us each by name.
God calls us, calls us, calls us
God calls us each by name.

God loves us, loves us, loves us
God loves us every day.
God loves us, loves us, loves us
God loves us every day.

We Are Happy to Serve the Lord

(tune: Mary Had a Little Lamb)
We are happy to serve the Lord,
serve the Lord,
serve the Lord.
We are happy to serve the Lord,
and help each other, too.

To make a pop-up puppet: Place the previous page over a cutting board and cut the figure of Samuel along the solid lines using a sharp art knife. Fold along the dotted line. If you wish, reinforce this fold with a piece of clear tape. Each time Samuel needs to stand up, lift the figure to the fold mark. Lay him flat when he is in bed.

Stories
from the
Greek Scriptures
(New Testament)

An Angel Visits Mary

Jeremiah 33:14-16
Luke 1:26-38

Use the figures of Mary and the angel from the fold-out cover to tell the story.

Jeremiah was a prophet who lived a long time ago – many years before Jesus was born. A prophet is a special messenger of God's word. Jeremiah told the people how God wanted them to live. Sometimes the people wouldn't listen! But that didn't stop Jeremiah. He told the people that God promised to send them a special leader. The people wanted their new leader now, but Jeremiah knew that they might have to wait a long time. They had to wait and hope.

Hundreds of years later, a woman named Mary was also waiting, just like Jeremiah. It all began when an angel visited Mary at her home in a town called Nazareth.

It was night and Mary was sitting quietly looking out of her window at the stars. Suddenly there was a beautiful light in the room. It grew and grew until Mary felt it all around her. It was an angel! The angel smiled at Mary and said, "Be happy, Mary! I have been sent by God to tell you that you are going to have a baby. His name will be Jesus. He will be the special leader God promised to send. He will show God's love to everyone."

Mary was surprised by what the angel said. But she said, "If God wants me to have this special baby, then that is what I will do."

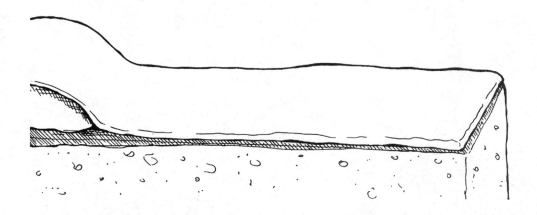

Advent Waiting Song

(tune: Mary Had a Little Lamb)
A-Advent is with us now,
with us now, with us now.
A-Advent is with us now,
Our wait-ing time is here.

We clap our hands with happy smiles,
happy smiles, happy smiles.
We clap our hands with happy smiles,
And wait for Baby Jesus.

We tiptoe 'round with lots of love,
lots of love, lots of love.
We tiptoe 'round with lots of love,
And wait for Baby Jesus.

Wave to friends with caring hearts,
caring hearts, caring hearts.
Wave to friends with caring hearts,
And wait for Baby Jesus.

We fold our hands and give God thanks,
give God thanks, give God thanks.
We fold our hands and give God thanks,
Thanks for Baby Jesus.

Prophet's Song

(tune: Twinkle, Twinkle Little Star)
Listen, listen to what I say,
someone special is on the way.
God says this to you and me
God says we must wait and see.
Listen, listen to what I say,
someone special is on the way!

I Am Waiting

(tune: Frère Jacques)
I am waiting. I am waiting.
On this day. On this day.
Jesus will be born soon. Jesus will be born soon.
On Christmas day. On Christmas day.

Is it time yet? Is it time yet?
Must I wait? Must I wait?
When is Jesus coming? When is Jesus coming?
It will be great. I can hardly wait.

I am joyful. I am joyful.
On this day. On this day.
Jesus will be born soon. Jesus will be born soon.
On Christmas day. On Christmas day.

An Angel Came to Mary

(tune: This Old Man)
An angel came
An angel came
To give good news to Ma-ary.
You're going to have a baby,
Jesus is his name,
He'll show God's love to everyone.

God Decided to Send a Son

(Clap hands on "I can hardly wait")
God decided to send a son. I can hardly wait.
Prophets said that he would come. I can hardly wait.
Joseph dreamed it in his bed. I can hardly wait.
"Don't be afraid," the angel said. I can hardly wait.
Yes, Mary was the chosen one. I can hardly wait.
Jesus was her little son. I can hardly wait.

Joseph and Mary's Journey

Luke 2:1-7

Use the figures of Mary and Joseph from the fold-out cover to tell this story. Use the drawing of the stable below.

Mary and Joseph had to go to Bethlehem, where Joseph had been born, because the king wanted to count everybody in his kingdom. They had walked and walked under the hot sun. Mary was going to have her baby soon. She was hot and tired and thirsty. She was happy to finally sit down. She asked Joseph, "How much further do we have to walk?"

Joseph smiled at Mary. He was tired too. "We're almost there, Mary. Maybe tonight we will arrive in Bethlehem." While they rested they wondered what it would be like to have a little baby to love and care for. They knew they wouldn't have long to wait now.

When they arrived in Bethlehem, Joseph looked for a place for them to stay. All the rooms were full. There was no room. But an innkeeper saw how sad Joseph looked and how tired Mary was. He said they could sleep in his stable with the animals. They found a corner and spread out their blankets. They lay on the straw, pulled the blankets over them, and held each other very close. They felt happy. They knew that their baby would be born soon.

Here We Go Up to Bethlehem

(tune: Mulberry Bush)
Here we go up to Bethlehem,
Bethlehem, Bethlehem.
Here we go up to Bethlehem,
on a long and tiring journey.

Where shall we stay in Bethlehem,
Bethlehem, Bethlehem?
Where shall we stay in Bethlehem,
on a long and tiring journey?

Other Verses

Let's stay in this stable it's safe and warm...
on our long and tiring journey.

Jesus was born in Bethlehem...
in a stable safe and warm.

Good news, good news, the angels sing...
for a special baby is born.

Sing songs of praise at Christmastime...
to God who gave us Jesus.

Here Is Joseph and Here Is Mary

Here is Joseph and here is Mary. *(raise two fingers)*
They come to an inn so tired and weary. *(two fingers walk)*
Knock, knock, knock. Please open your door. *(knock)*
The innkeeper says, "There's no room for more." *(shake head)*
They walk and they walk till the end of the day. *(two fingers walk)*
Where they find a stable and a bed of hay. *(hands make roof)*
And there in the stable on Christmas morn,
Jesus the son of God was born. *(cradle arms)*

Jesus Is Born

Luke 2:8-20

Use the figures of Mary, Joseph, Donkey, and Manger from the fold-out cover, and the illustration of the stable from p. 28, to tell this story.

It was the night that Mary's baby was born. Mary and Joseph were so happy! Joseph found a manger that was filled with hay for the animals to eat. "This will make a good bed for our baby Jesus," he said. Mary lovingly wrapped baby Jesus in strips of cloth and laid him down to sleep.

On a hillside nearby, shepherds looked after their sheep. Suddenly there was a bright light. Angels sang, and told the shepherds, "A special baby has been born in Bethlehem. He is the one God promised to send. He will show God's love to everyone."

The shepherds were so excited they went to Bethlehem right away. They found Mary and Joseph in the stable. Baby Jesus was lying in a manger, just as the angels said. The shepherds welcomed the baby and thanked God for this wonderful night and this special baby.

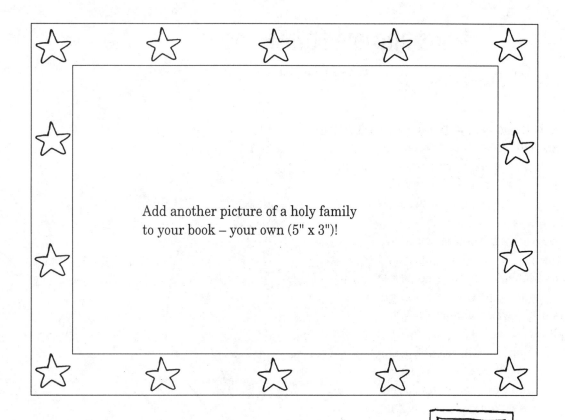

Add another picture of a holy family
to your book – your own (5" x 3")!

Away in a Manger

Away in a manger,
No crib for a bed. *(cradle arms)*
The little Lord Jesus,
Laid down his sweet head. *(fold hands and put
under ear like pillow)*
The stars in the bright sky
Looked down where he lay. *(point up then shade
eyes and look down)*
The little Lord Jesus,
Asleep on the hay. *(rock baby)*

Make a pan flute from drinking straws
(see p. 11) to accompany this song!

Here's a Tiny Little Bed

Here's a tiny little bed. *(cup hand)*
Here's a tiny little head. *(lay finger in cupped
hand)*
Shhh! Baby Jesus is sleeping. *(put finger to
mouth)*

Baby Jesus Is Born

(tune: The Bear Went over the Mountain)
Baby Jesus is bo-rn.
Baby Jesus is bo-rn.
Baby Jesus is bo-rn.
He came for you and me!
He came so we would see,
how loving we can be.
Baby Jesus is bo-rn.
Baby Jesus is bo-rn.
Baby Jesus is bo-rn.
Thank God! Thank God! Thank God!

Towel Baby Jesus

Make a towel doll (see p. 19).
Children will love having their
own Baby Jesus to retell the
story with!

Jesus and the Four Fishers

Luke 5:1-11

Hello, my name is Peter. I am a friend of Jesus. One day, when I had been fishing all night with my friends, Andrew, James and John, Jesus came walking along the sand. We were tired and we were putting our nets away when Jesus asked if he could sit in our boat to teach the people who had gathered to listen to him. So we got in the boat and rowed out on the water.

When Jesus finished teaching the people, he asked us to go out to the deeper water and throw our nets in the water again. We had been fishing all night and hadn't caught anything. Not one fish! But we trusted Jesus, so we did what he asked. We rowed the boat out to deep water and threw our nets out one more time. When we pulled our nets back in, they were full of fish!

Jesus had helped us do our work. Then Jesus asked us to come and help him with his work. So Andrew, James, and John and I left our boat and followed Jesus. We traveled with him from town to town. We helped him teach people about God's love.

How many fish can you count?

The Four Fishers

(tune: London Bridge)
Andrew, Peter, James and John,
James and John, James and John,
Andrew, Peter, James and John,
Followed Jesus.
(After you've sung it several times, substitute the children's names for those of the disciples.)

Four Friends

Four friends were working *(hold up four fingers)*
One day by the sea,
And heard someone calling
"Come follow me." *(beckon with hand)*
It was Jesus who called them,
Each by name, *(hands cupped to mouth)*
Peter, Andrew, John and James. *(hold up four fingers, one at a time)*

Yes, Jesus Calls Me

(tune: chorus of Jesus Loves Me)
Yes, Jesus calls me,
Yes, Jesus calls me,
Yes, Jesus calls me,
To follow him today.

Deep Blue Sea

(tune: One Little, Two Little, Three Little...)
One little, two little, three little fishes
Four little, five little, six little fishes
Seven little, eight little, nine little fishes
Down in the deep blue sea.

Additional verses:
Andrew, Peter and James in a sailboat...*(3x)*
And John on the deep blue sea.

Jesus their friend came down to see them...*(3x)*
Down by the deep blue sea.

Jesus asked them all to follow...*(3x)*
Down by the deep blue sea.

Follow Me

(tune: Mary Had a Little Lamb)
Jesus said, "Come follow me,
follow me, follow me."
Jesus said, "Come follow me,
and help me spread God's love."

Jesus Blesses The Children

Mark 10:13-16

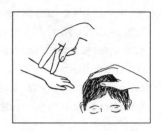

Ask the child to extend their hand, palm open. As you tell the story make a "walking" motion in the palm of the child's hand. "Walk" fingers up the arm to the child's shoulder. Place your hand on the child's shoulder or head to bless them as you tell how Jesus blessed the children.

There was a family who wanted to meet Jesus. Early in the morning, they started walking. They had a long way to go. They walked and walked. The children were tired. Finally they saw a crowd of people. It must be Jesus!

They ran to see him but they could not get close. There were too many big people. The children couldn't see anything! They started to cry. They said, "We want to see Jesus, too!"

Some of Jesus' disciples told the children to go away. They said, "Stop bothering Jesus. He's too busy to see you now."

But when Jesus saw the children, he smiled. He said, "Don't push the children away. I want to see them. Everyone, especially children, belongs to God's family. Children are the smallest people in God's family yet they are filled with God's joy and love. We all can learn about living in God's way from them."

Then Jesus gave each child a big hug. He laid his hand gently on their heads and blessed them, saying, "You are an important part of God's family. God loves you. I love you."

The children loved Jesus, too.

Jesus Is Coming

"Jesus is coming. Let's go and see." *(beckon with hand)*

So we walked, and we ran, as fast as could be. *(walk and run on the spot)*

Too many people, we can't see! *(shade eyes and look around)*

"Go away," some said. "Jesus is busy!" *(cross arms over chest as if angry)*

But then we heard kind Jesus say, *(put hand to ear)*

I love the children – let them stay!

Let them come and talk to me. *(hold arms out invitingly)*

So we ran, and we jumped up on his knee! *(pat knees)*

B-L-E-S-S

(tune: Bingo)

Blessings make me warm inside,

They make me want to giggle!

B-L-E-S-S

(clap, clap, clap, clap, clap as you say each letter)

B-L-E-S-S

(clap as you say each letter)

B-L-E-S-S

(clap as you say each letter)

You bless us every day.

(Sing the verse again, leaving out the letter "B" and replacing it with a clap. Then leave out both the "B" and the "L." Repeat the song until you have replaced all the letters with claps.)

God Has Blessed Me

(tune: Fire's Burning)

God has blessed me, God has blessed me,

God loves me, God loves me.

I will share God's

love with others

God has blessed me, God has blessed me.

God Blesses Us

(tune: Twinkle, Twinkle Little Star)

God blesses us and loves us, too.

This is what we all can do,

Try to be loving, kind and fair,

Share God's blessing everywhere.

God blesses us and loves us, too

This is what we all can do.

The Lost Coin

Luke 15:8-10

One day, Jesus told his friends a story about a woman who had ten silver coins. (Let's call her Sarah.) These coins were very special to Sarah. To keep her coins safe, Sarah had sewn each one of them onto the edge of a head scarf she wore every day.

One morning, Sarah noticed that her head scarf felt different. Quickly she began to count the coins on her scarf. "1, 2, 3, 4, 5, 6, 7, 8, 9...9? Let me count again. 1, 2, 3, 4, 5, 6, 7, 8, 9... Oh no! One is missing!" Imagine how Sarah felt. Her coins were very special to her.

Sarah looked around the room to see if she could find the lost coin. She lit a candle and began to hunt for it everywhere in her home. She hunted under the bed. She hunted behind the dishes in her cupboards. She looked through her sewing basket and dumped out everything that was inside. She could not find her coin anywhere so she decided to sweep her entire house. Around and around she swept. She swept and swept until she had swept her whole house. Suddenly she spotted it. She was so excited that she danced right on the spot!

Jesus told this story to help people understand how special we are to God. If we have lost our way God will search for us until we are found, just as the woman hunted for her coin. We are that precious to God!

Can you find the missing coin? Help Sarah count all 10!

I'm a Special Person

(tune: I'm a Little Teapot)
I'm a special person,
You are, too.
God loves me,
And God loves you.

God Is with Us

(tune: God Is with Us)
God is with us,
God is with us,
God is with us, everywhere.

God's Love Is

(tune: God's Love Is)
God's love is –
So high you can't get over it,
So low you can't get under it,
So wide you can't get around it,
God's love is everywhere.

The Good Samaritan

Luke 10:30-37

Use the figure of the Donkey from the fold-out cover to tell this story. Place the Donkey in front of the figure of the wounded man as you tell how the Samaritan helped him.

A man (let's call him Thomas) was walking along the road one day. Suddenly, some robbers sneaked up behind him and stole everything he had! They hurt Thomas very badly and left him lying on the road. He couldn't get up. All he could do was lie there and wait for someone to help him.

He waited and he waited. Finally, he could see a man coming. "Thank goodness!" he thought. But when the man saw Thomas lying on the road, the man looked away and kept right on walking. Thomas called out, "Please help me! Some robbers have hurt me and taken everything I own!" But the man pretended he could not hear Thomas.

Thomas waited and waited. He was cold now and hungry and thirsty. His cuts and bruises were aching. Finally, he saw another man coming. Thomas cried out, "Please help me! Some robbers have hurt me and taken everything I own!" But the man pretended not to hear Thomas. He was afraid that the men who had robbed Thomas might be waiting to rob him, too.

Thomas felt so alone. Who would be a good neighbor? Who would stop and help him? Then he saw a man coming towards him. The man was from Samaria. Jewish people and Samaritans didn't usually want to have anything to do with each other, so Thomas was surprised when the man rushed over to see what was wrong. The kind Samaritan said, "Let me help you!"

The Samaritan gently put bandages on his cuts. Then he lifted Thomas onto his donkey and took him to an inn nearby. The Samaritan gave the innkeeper some money and said, "Please take good care of my new friend. Keep him warm. Give him lots of food and drinks. I will give you some money for a doctor to look at his cuts."

Thomas got better very quickly. He never forgot the good Samaritan. Whenever he told this story he said, "The Samaritan was a true neighbor to me. He showed me how to share God's love with others."

God Is Pleased

(tune: Mulberry Bush)
God is pleased when we share what we have,
Share what we have, share what we have.
God is pleased when we share what we have,
So that's what we will do.

Other verses:
sing and pray
make new friends
care for others

The Helpers

Two little eyes to see things to do
   (point to eyes)
Two little lips to smile the day through
   (point to lips)
Two little ears to hear what you say
   (point to ears)
Two little hands to put our toys away
   (extend hands in front)
A mouth to speak kind words each day
   (point to mouth)
A loving heart for work and play
   (hands over heart)
Two feet that errands gladly run
   (point to feet)
Make happy days for everyone.
   (smile)

This Little Hand

This little hand is a helping hand. *(hold out hand)*
This little hand is another. *(hold out other hand)*
Together they play, together they work,
And each one helps the other. *(fold in prayer position)*

A Troubled Man Is Helped

Mark 1:21-28

Where it says "pause", invite children to choose the face that expresses the emotions at that point in the story.

The people walked quickly to the synagogue. The synagogue is where the Jewish people went to worship God. "Why is everyone hurrying?" a child asked.

"Jesus is teaching at the synagogue!" someone answered. "Let's go!" (Pause)

Soon the synagogue was filled with people who wanted to hear what Jesus was saying. Many people whispered to each other. "He loves God very much. He makes me feel close to God. I could listen to him teach all day." People moved closer to hear every word Jesus said. They knew that Jesus was a special leader sent by God. (Pause)

Suddenly, there was a lot of noise at the back of the synagogue. (Pause) A man came forward screaming, "Jesus of Nazareth! Jesus of Nazareth!" The man was so loud that the people couldn't hear Jesus anymore. (Pause) They complained to each other. "Who is this noisy person? What does he want? This man seems very upset and confused. What should we do? He is getting louder by the minute. Should we make him leave?" The people were so worried about what they should do, they didn't notice Jesus walking toward the man. (Pause)

"Look, Jesus is going to him. What do you think he will do? Will he make him leave the synagogue? Maybe Jesus will scold him for being so noisy." Everyone watched to see what Jesus would do.

Jesus knew that the man had an illness that made him say and do some strange things. Jesus laid his hands gently on the man's head and spoke some words. Right away the man became calm and quiet. He felt God's love all around him. Jesus helped the man to know that he was welcome in the synagogue and that he belonged there, too. (Pause)

Jesus Helps, I Can Help

(tune: Hush Li'l Baby – The Mockingbird Song)
Jesus helps us when we're sad.
Jesus helps us when we're mad.
Jesus helps us night and day.
Jesus helps us know God's way.

I can help you when you're sad.
I can help you when you're mad.
I can help you night and day.
Jesus helps me live God's way.

What Shall We Do?

(tune: What Shall We Do?)
What shall we do to help another
What shall we do to help another
What shall we do to help another
That will serve God gladly?

Other verse suggestions:
Let's all smile and say come join us...
Make new friends and care for others...

Jesus Loves Each One

(tune: Kum Ba Yah)
Jesus loves each one, you and me.
Jesus loves each one as family.
Jesus loves each one, so you see,
The world is God's community.

The Widow and the Judge

Luke 18:1-8

Children will pick up the pattern of the story very quickly. Encourage them to say the verses with you.

There once was a widow. She lived all by herself. Her husband had died and she had no children. She was very poor. One day she went to see the judge. A neighbor had been unfair to her. She wanted the judge to put things right. She said to the judge,

> Knock, knock
> Please listen to me!
> I need your help, Judge
> Can't you see?

The judge did not care about her. He would not listen to her story. He said,

> Go away!
> Can't you see?
> Your problem doesn't
> matter to me.

But the woman would not give up. Every day she would go to the judge's house and say,

> Knock, knock
> Please listen to me!
> I need your help, Judge
> Can't you see?

And every day the judge would say,

> Go away!
> Can't you see?
> Your problem doesn't
> matter to me.

Over and over the woman asked the judge to make things fair. She would say,

> Knock, knock
> Please listen to me!
> I need your help, Judge
> Can't you see?

And the judge would say,

> Go away!
> Can't you see?
> Your problem doesn't
> matter to me.

But still the woman would not give up. Finally, he said, "That's enough! Please stop bothering me!" The uncaring judge changed his mind because the woman would not give up. So the judge said,

> You didn't give up
> You tried and tried.
> I'll help you now
> I'll take your side.

The woman had been so persistent! That means she kept trying and trying. She kept on speaking out and asking to be heard. We can be persistent, too, in loving God and other people.

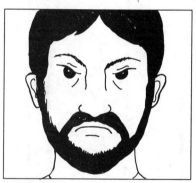

Option: Cut a square of paper to fit over the judge. Fold a tab and tape along edge. Children can open the door each time the widow knocks, and close the door each time they hear the judge's response.

I Can Pray to God

(tune: Jesus Loves Me)
I can pray to God all day
if I'm working or at play
When I'm happy or I'm sad
God is with me, I am glad.
Yes, God will hear me
Yes, God will hear me
Yes, God will hear me
So I'll pray to God each day.

Thank God

(tune: Thank God)
Thank God, thank God,
Thanks in the morning,
Thanks at the noontime,
Thank God, Thank God,
Thanks when the sun goes down.

Other verses:

Praise God, Serve God, Love God, etc. Add your own...

The Persistence Song

(tune: Row, Row, Row Your Boat)
Per-sistence is a word
so very hard to say
Try and try and try again
and then you'll know the way
Per-sistence is a word
so very hard to say
It means to try and try again
in school, in prayer and play.

Nicodemus Comes to See Jesus
John 3:1-21

Use a flashlight when telling this story at bedtime or to create the impression of day and night.

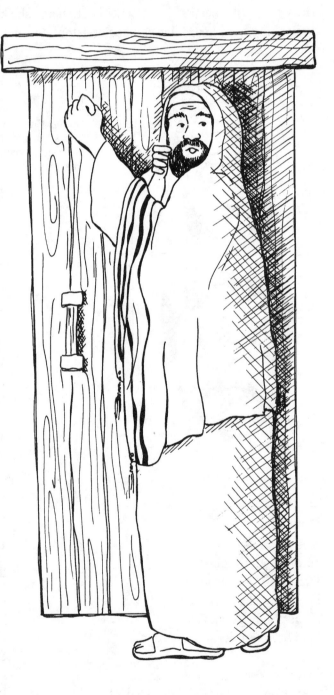

Nicodemus was an important teacher. Late one night, when it was very dark, Nicodemus came to see Jesus. He didn't want anyone to know about his visit. He was afraid people might laugh at him. He walked quickly and quietly through the streets until he reached the house where Jesus was staying. He knocked on the door. The door opened and Jesus was standing there. *(Turn on flashlight.)*

"Come in," Jesus said.

Nicodemus looked behind him *(turn off flashlight)* to see if anyone saw him and then he went inside. *(Turn on flashlight.)*

"Jesus," said Nicodemus, "I know you are a teacher sent by God. Teach me more about God."

Jesus smiled at Nicodemus and said, "When you really know God, it is like beginning life all over again. God's love is like a light that shines on things so you can see them clearly. Some people don't like that. They want to hide the wrong things they do. But if you know God's love, then you know God forgives you. God helps us change and grow."

Nicodemus wondered about what Jesus had told him. He was glad he came to see Jesus. As he left the house, Nicodemus felt like a new person. Jesus had helped him see and understand God in a new way. *(Turn off flashlight.)*

This Little Light of Mine

(tune: This Little Light of Mine)
This little light of mine,
I'm going to let it shine.
This little light of mine,
I'm going to let it shine.
This little light of mine,
I'm going to let it shine.
Let it shine, let it shine, let it shine.

Other verses:
Hide it behind my back – no way!
I'm going to let it shine...

I won't let anyone "whiff" (blow) it out
I'm going to let it shine...

Going to shine right here in my hometown
I'm going to let it shine...

See the light spreading 'round the world
See all the faces shine...

Shining with God's Love

(tune: Jesus Loves Me)
Look at me, you'll see God's light
shining in my eyes so bright.
Look at me, you'll see God live
in all the love that I can give.

Chorus:
God's light is in me.
God's love is in me.
God's light is in me,
for all the world to see.

Jesus Heals Ten Men

Luke 17:11-19

Children might like to put a bandage on their finger as you tell this story of Jesus' healing.

Once there were ten people who were very sick. *(Hold up ten fingers.)* The people had a terrible skin disease. Because of the disease they had sores all over and they had to wear bandages all over their bodies. *(Wrap a finger with a bandage.)* Other people were afraid of them, so they had to leave their homes and families. They were very sad.

One day, Jesus was walking along the road. As he neared a town, he met those ten people. They called out to Jesus, "Jesus, have mercy on us." That means "help us." When Jesus saw them he said, "Go and show yourselves to the priests." As the ten men went off *(wiggle fingers as if they are walking)* something amazing happened! They were healed. They weren't sick anymore! *(Remove bandage or draw a happy face on it with a felt pen.)*

The men ran quickly to see the priests, so the priests could see that they were healed. But one of them stopped. He decided to go back and see Jesus. When he came close to Jesus he knelt down and said, "Thank you for helping me become well."

Jesus was glad the man had remembered to give God thanks.

Which man do you think came back to thank Jesus?

I Can Pray to God

(tune: Jesus Love Me)

I can pray to God all day,
If I'm working or at play.
When I'm happy or I'm sad,
God is with me, I am glad.
Yes, God will hear me
Yes, God will hear me
Yes, God will hear me
So I'll pray to God all day.

We Are in God's Family

(tune: This Old Man)

I see you. You see me.
We are in God's family.
As we live and grow and find new ways to be.
God's loving care for you and me.

We Fold Our Hands

(tune: Mary Had a Little Lamb)

We fold our hands and give God thanks,
Give God thanks, give God thanks.
We fold our hands and give God thanks,
Each and every day.

The Story of Jesus' Passion

Waving the Palm Branches
Mark 11:1-10

Use the figure of the Donkey from the fold-out cover. Place the donkey under Jesus.

I was so excited! I was in Jerusalem. I saw Jesus ride into the city on a donkey while his followers walked beside him. The people were very excited when they heard that Jesus was coming. They waved leafy palm branches and put their coats on the ground. They were very happy to see Jesus. They shouted "Hosanna! Hosanna! Hurray for Jesus!"

A Gift for Jesus
John 12:1-8

As you tell this story, rub a small amount of baby/bath oil or cooking oil on the child's hand.

My name is Mary. I am a friend of Jesus. Jesus came to my house for dinner.

Jesus told us that soon we wouldn't see him anymore. I was very sad.

To show him how much I loved him, I poured some special perfumed oil on his feet. Some people were angry with me. They said, "You are wasting oil that costs a lot of money! We could sell it and give the money to the poor. You shouldn't do that!"

But Jesus understood. He told them to leave me alone. He said, "Thank you. You will be remembered for this fine and beautiful blessing you have given me."

Songs and Fingerplays for Holy Week

See the instructions on p. 12 for making simple rhythm instruments to accompany these songs.

This Is the Way

(tune: Mulberry Bush)
This is the way that Jesus came,
Jesus came, Jesus came.
This is the way that Jesus came,
Riding on a donkey.

Palm Sunday Song

(tune: What Shall We Do?)
This is the way that Jesus came,
This is the way that Jesus came,
This is the way that Jesus came,
Riding on a donkey.

Let's all cheer and shout Hosanna,
Let's all cheer and shout Hosanna,
Let's all cheer and shout Hosanna,
Jesus is our king!

Jesus is Leading Us

(tune: Mary Had a Little Lamb)
Jesus is leading us on the way,
on the way, on the way,
Jesus is leading us on the way,
On our way to Easter.

Quiet Praying Time

(tune: I'm a Little Teapot)
I like quiet praying time *(fold hands in prayer)*
You will, too. *(point to another)*
God hears me *(point to self)*
And God hears you. *(point to another)*

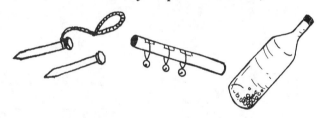

Sharing a Meal

Mark 14:12-26

I am a busy, busy man. Today was an important day! Jesus and his disciples came to my house to eat a special holiday meal. I bought special bread and wine for them to share. It was exciting to meet Jesus. I had heard all about the things he has done. Before they ate, they prayed, "Thank you God, for this time together." As Jesus passed the bread and wine to his friends he told them to remember him whenever they shared bread and wine together.

In the Garden
Mark 14:32-42

I was one of Jesus' friends. I was there the night we ate the special meal together.

When we finished eating, Jesus asked us to go with him to one of his favorite quiet places to pray. It was late at night when we got there. I tried hard to stay awake and pray but I felt so tired.

Suddenly we heard shouts. We didn't know what was happening. There were torches and soldiers everywhere.

Then I saw soldiers grab Jesus and tie his hands together. They arrested him and were going to take him away. I was confused and frightened. I ran away because I was afraid I would be arrested, too.

The Three Crosses
Mark 15:21-47

Give children a small stone to hold while you tell this story.

Early the next morning the people who were angry with Jesus asked that he be put to death. I was there with the other friends of Jesus' when he was put on a cross and he died. When Jesus died, we all felt very sad. We wrapped Jesus' body in soft white cloth and laid him in a cave in a garden. A big stone was rolled across the opening of the cave. Then we went home because we didn't know what else to do.

The Empty Tomb
Mark 16:1-8

Use the figure of the Angel from the fold-out cover to tell this story. Place the angel in front of the tomb.

Three days after Jesus died, on Easter Sunday, some of us women came to the garden where they had buried Jesus. When we got there, we found the stone rolled away. Jesus' body was gone! Then we saw an angel – a messenger from God who told us, "Don't be sad. God has given Jesus new life. Jesus is alive again, and will be with you." We were so surprised and full of joy! This is what we celebrate on Easter day!

Songs for Easter

See instructions on pp. 11-12 for making simple rhythm instruments to accompany these songs.

Alleluia
(tune: Frère Jacques)
Alleluia. Alleluia.
Praise God! Praise God!
Je-sus is risen, Je-sus is risen,
He's with us again! He's with us again!

Happy Easter, Happy Easter,
Praise God! Praise God!
We're an Easter people, We're an Easter people
Praise God! Praise God!

Easter Song
(tune: Mulberry Bush)
What do we do at Eastertime?
At Eastertime, Eastertime?
What do we do at Eastertime?
We sing our songs for Jesus.

We clap our hands and sing Allelu
Sing Allelu, sing Allelu
We clap our hands and sing Allelu
Sing Allelu for Jesus.

Ho, Ho, Ho Hosanna
(tune: Early One Morning – Friendly Giant tune)
Ho, Ho, Ho Hosanna
Ha, Ha, Hallelujah
He, He, He is risen
Praise his holy name.

The Disciples Believe

Luke 24:13-48

Cleopas and his friend were running along a dark road. They wanted to get to Jerusalem as soon as possible. They wanted to tell the other disciples that Jesus is alive again – they had talked with him. They had eaten with him!

When they got to Jerusalem, the other disciples didn't believe them. Not at first. Cleopas kept saying, "But we saw him ourselves. Can't you believe us?" The other disciples wanted to believe. But how could Jesus be alive when he died on the cross?

Then all of a sudden, Jesus was there in the room with them. "Hello friends," he said. "Don't be afraid. It's really me!"

Jesus' friends could hardly believe it was him. He said, "Touch me and see that I am alive." They touched him. He was real.

"Wow!" they said. "You are alive."

"I'm alive," said Jesus. "And I'd like something to eat."

They shared some fish and had a long, long talk. They laughed and told stories. Jesus told them, "God loves you. When you do wrong and you say 'I'm sorry' to God, God will forgive you. God will help you to try again to live in God's way." This was good news for the disciples to hear. It was the good news that Jesus wanted them to share with everyone.

Good News Song

(tune: Mulberry Bush)
Jesus is with us every day,
every day, every day.
Jesus is with us every day.
Good News! Good News! Good News!

God's love for me will always stay,
always stay, always stay.
God's love for me will always stay.
Good News! Good News! Good News!

Jesus Is with Us

This is the house where I live.
My family lives here, too.
Jesus is with us all the time,
And helps us in all we do.

We never really see him, *(hand to forehead
searching)*
But we know he's always there.
For we feel that he is loving us *(hug self)*
And we know his gentle care.

Share Good News

(tune: Frère Jacques)
Jesus loves us. Jesus loves us.
Share Good News. Share Good News.
He is always with us,
and will never leave us,
Share Good News. Share Good News.

Lydia Starts a Church

Acts 16:9-15

Lydia and her friends loved God. There was no worship building where they lived, so they gathered at the river to pray.

One day they met two disciples named Paul and Silas. Paul and Silas told Lydia and the other women about Jesus. Lydia was very excited.

"That is good news," Lydia said to Paul. "Jesus came to show us that we're all part of God's family! I want to tell everyone!"

Then Lydia said, "Paul, I feel the spirit of God in me. I want to be a follower of Jesus, too. Would you baptize me?" So Paul baptized Lydia in the river. When Lydia came up out of the water she felt God all around her. Soon all of Lydia's family was baptized.

Lydia invited Paul and Silas to stay at her house. Many people came to hear about Jesus. It was so warm and friendly at Lydia's house! Everyone would meet there to talk about Jesus and eat together. They remembered that Jesus said, "Every time you eat bread and drink wine together, remember me."

Many people were baptized and became followers of Jesus. And Lydia became the leader of a brand new house church.

The Church Is One Big Family

(tune: London Bridge)
The church is one big family, family, family,
The church is one big family,
The church is everywhere.

And in this family of love, family of love, family of love
And in this family of love,
I know that I belong.

Here Is the Church

Here is the church,
Here is the steeple,
Open the door,
See all the people.

Close the doors,
And hear them pray.
They're learning to follow
in Jesus' way.

Open the doors,
They're on their way,
To share God's love
With others each day.

The Church Is Everywhere

The church is one big family. *(join hands)*
The church is everywhere. *(open arms wide)*
It's people tall, and people small. *(show height)*
The church is folk who share. *(turn to another and hold out hands)*

And in this family of love
I know that I belong. *(join hands)*
The church is people loving *(smile at each other)*
Through helping, prayer and song. *(bow heads and fold hands)*

God's Spirit

We can't see the wind
But we know it's there
'Cause it rustles the leaves
And blows our hair.
God's spirit is with us
We know that's true
And people can see it
In the things that we do.

Invite children to act out a baptism, using a doll and a basin of water. Show them how to make the sign of a cross on the doll's head and say, "You are part of God's family."

Away in a Manger

Bingo

What Shall We Do? (Drunken Sailor)

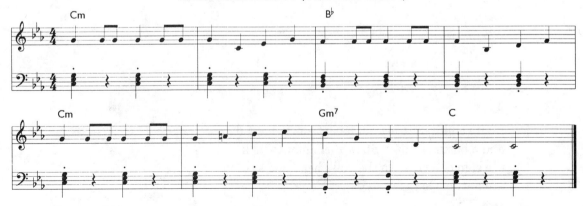

Fire's Burning

Frère Jacques

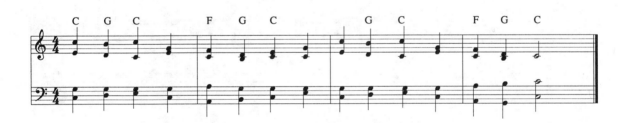

God Is with Us

God's Love Is

Hush Li'l Baby

If You're Happy

I'm a Little Teapot

Itsy Bitsy Spider

Jesus Loves Me

Kum Ba Yah

London Bridge

Mary Had a Little Lamb

One Little, Two Little, Three Little

Paw Paw Patch

Ring Around the Rosy

Row, Row, Row Your Boat

Thank God

Three Blind Mice

The Bear Went over the Mountain

This Little Light of Mine

Twinkle, Twinkle Little Star

Hey La-di, La-di, La-di

Mulberry Bush

This Old Man

Early One Morning (Friendly Giant)

INDEX

(BY THEME)